ALLIGATORS ARE AWFUL

(and they have terrible manners, too)

by David McPhail

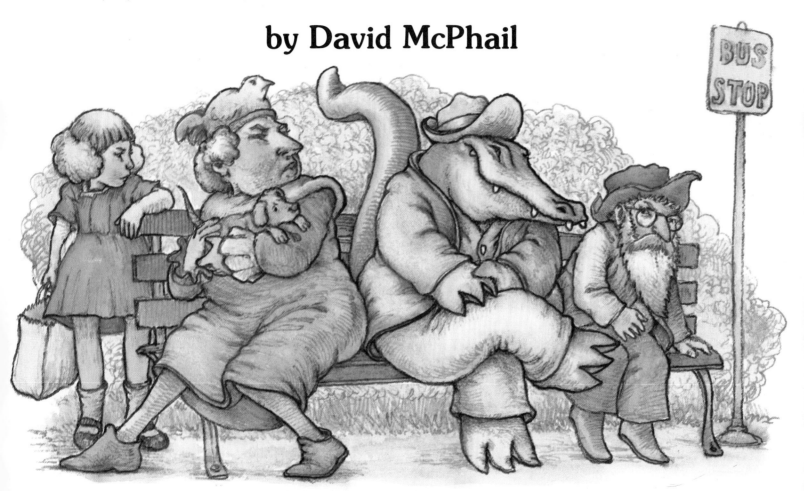

Doubleday & Company, Inc., Garden City, New York

Alligators are awful.
Simply awful!

Library of Congress Catalog Card Number 79-7607

ISBN:0-385-13582-3 Trade   ISBN: 0-385-13583-1 Prebound Copyright © 1980 by David McPhail
All Rights Reserved   Printed in the United States of America   First Edition

They are rude, too.
If you ask them
a question,
they just snort.

They sit in front of you at the movies and never take off their hats.

When you are
having a soda
at the ice-cream
parlor, they blow their
straw papers at you.

Alligators are pushy, too.
When the bus finally comes,
they always have to be the
first one on.

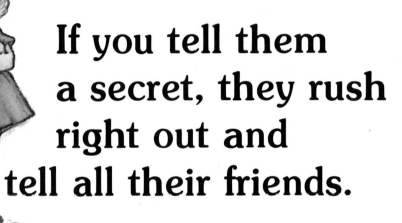

If you tell them
a secret, they rush
right out and
tell all their friends.

After you've spent the whole afternoon raking your front yard, they jump in the pile of leaves and scatter them all over.

When you're
waiting in the rain to
cross the street,
they go speeding by and
splash you.

If you let them
ride your tricycle,
they get their tails caught
and break the spokes.

When you get a new book, those awful alligators look over your shoulder, and they won't let you turn the page until they have read it.

And what terrible table manners alligators have. When it's your birthday they never wait for you to make a wish and blow out the candles.

They talk
for hours on the phone
when somebody has to
make a call.

Oh, those awful alligators!

I'm certainly glad that *people* aren't like those awful alligators!